My Brother, Micky and His Icky, Sticky Hands

My Brother, Micky and His Icky, Sticky Hands

BY **Dawn M. DiDominzio**

ILLUSTRATED BY **Gia Brock**

To the beautiful, little flower, Autumn Rose

My name is Lily, and I have a little brother named Micky.

I'm thinking my mom should have named him icky, or maybe, sticky.

Here's why...

Like - when I'm looking in the mirror combing my curls, only to find Micky's icky, sticky handprints smiling back at me.

Or, when – I'm cleaning my hands, only to find Micky's icky, sticky fingerprints all over the clean, white towel.

Or maybe - when I'm opening the refrigerator, only to find Micky's icky, sticky handprints going up and down the handle.

They are even on some of the food!

YUCK!

Can anyone else see?

It's because of Micky and his icky, sticky hands!

Just like when Micky brought home his school paper with a fancy, blue, silk ribbon on it.

It was the 1st Place Art Award!

Didn't his teacher see?

It' was just my brother and his icky, sticky
hands!

On Mother's Day, my mom was delighted about her once ordinary coffee mug having "flowers" on it from left to right.

Courtesy of... Micky

Didn't my mom see?

It was just Micky and his icky, sticky hands!

My birthday party was great, but my friends
kept talking about the "Butterfly" balloons...
I really love butterflies, but –

Didn't they see?

It was just my brother and his icky, sticky hands!

One week ago, our brand new community park opened and everyone gathered and cheered when they saw the wall mural by –

You guessed it

Micky...

... and his not so magical hands!

Didn't they see?

It was just my brother and his icky, sticky hands!

Yesterday, the Bakersfield Zoo opened - complete with my brother's so called art on their welcome sign.

Didn't they see?

It was just my brother and his icky, sticky hands!

This morning at the Pumpkin Decorating Festival, everyone thought Micky's "ghosts" were really cute.

Didn't they see?

It was just my brother and his icky, sticky hands!

Well, that was the last straw! Do you want to know what I am going to do?

I'm going to march into his room and tell him that I know all about those non-art-making hands of his...

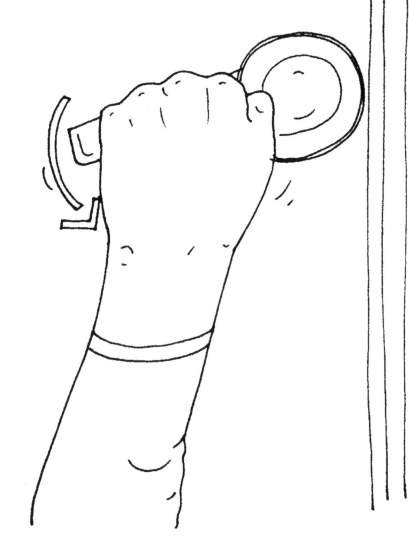

I can't believe what I am seeing with my very own two eyes!

My brother really is an artist!

The **icky, sticky** artist, that is!

"I am so proud of you, Micky."

"I always knew you had talent."

The End

66581866R00020

Made in the USA
Charleston, SC
24 January 2017